KORGI

CREATED BY

ANN & CHRISTIAN SLADE

top
Shelf
PRODUCTIONS

CHRISTIAN SLADE

BOOK 4

TOP SHELF PRODUCTIONS

KORGI (BOOK 4): THE PROBLEM WITH POTIONS © 2016 CHRISTIAN SLADE.

Published by Top Shelf Productions, PO Box 1282, Marietta, GA 30061-1282, USA. Top Shelf Productions is an imprint of IDW Publishing, a division of Idea and Design Works, LLC. Offices: 2765 Truxtun Road, San Diego, CA 92106. Top Shelf Productions®, the Top Shelf logo, Idea and Design Works®, and the IDW logo are registered trademarks of Idea and Design Works, LLC. All Rights Reserved. With the exception of small excerpts of artwork used for review purposes, none of the contents of this publication may be reprinted without the permission of IDW Publishing. IDW Publishing does not read or accept unsolicited submissions of ideas, stories, or artwork.

Editor-in-Chief: Chris Staros.

Visit our online catalog at www.topshelfcomix.com.

Printed in Korea.

ISBN 978-1-60309-403-0

20   19   18   17   16   5   4   3   2   1

Thanks to Chris Staros
and the Top Shelf family.

Fellow artist friends Brad Tabar,
Ken Banks, Mike Brady, Joe Fauvel,
Ray Richardson, and James Dalton.

Janice Fauste, Deb Shindle,
Kandee Bishea, Thyra Harris, Art Smith,
and all the corgi people who have
supported my work over the years.

Special thanks to my family,
especially Mom, Dad, Maggie, and David.

Extra special thanks to
Kate, Nate, and my wonderful wife, Ann.

Penny, Leo, Queenie, Will, Wanda, Apollo,
and all the Welsh Corgis in the world.

Thank you
for helping me find Korgi!

4

Have I Got the strangest tale for you today!

Sprout gets all mixed up in this book,
and, as usual, those Creephogs are involved!

They just cannot seem to leave Sprout alone. Of course, it is not
the Creephogs' fault. They have to obey their master,
the terrible Derog-Glaw, who desperately needs a fire-breather
like Sprout in order to reverse the magic that long ago
fused those two brothers into a two-headed monster.

Be sure to keep a lookout for me as well,
as I continue to watch out over this Korgi Hollow.

Welcome back to the world of Korgi, dear reader!
This is Book 4 and a tale I call...

"The Problem with Potions!"

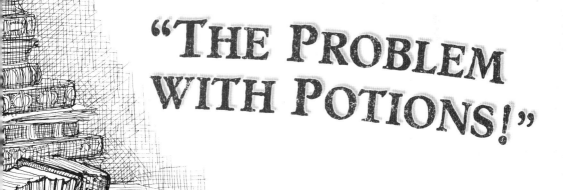

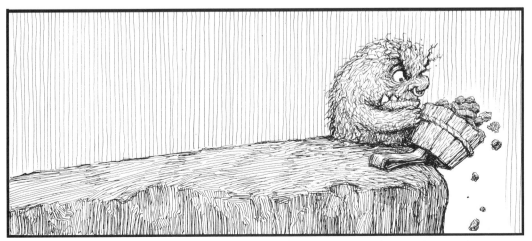

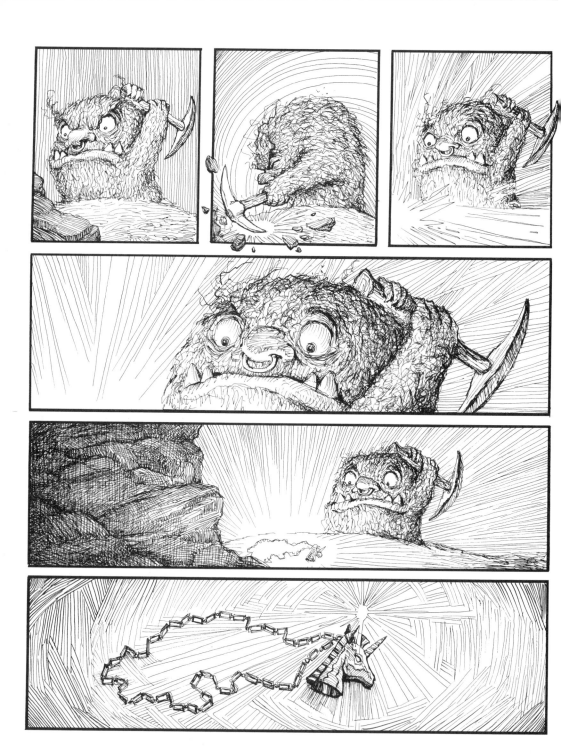

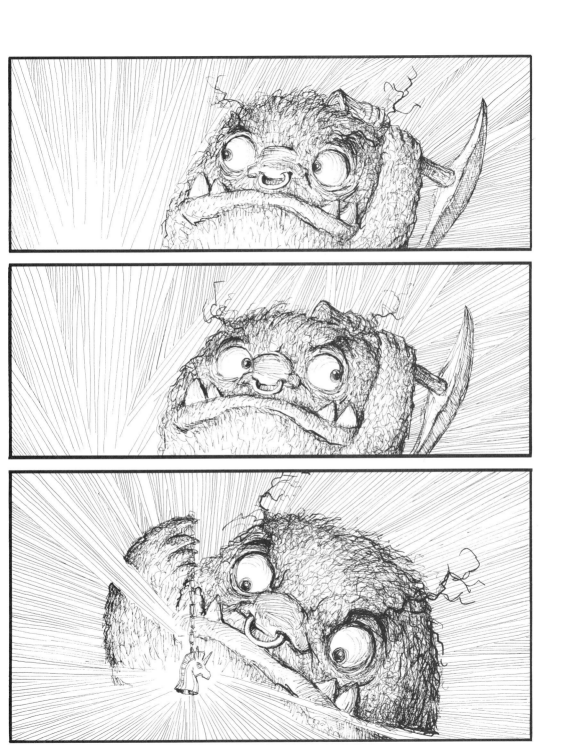

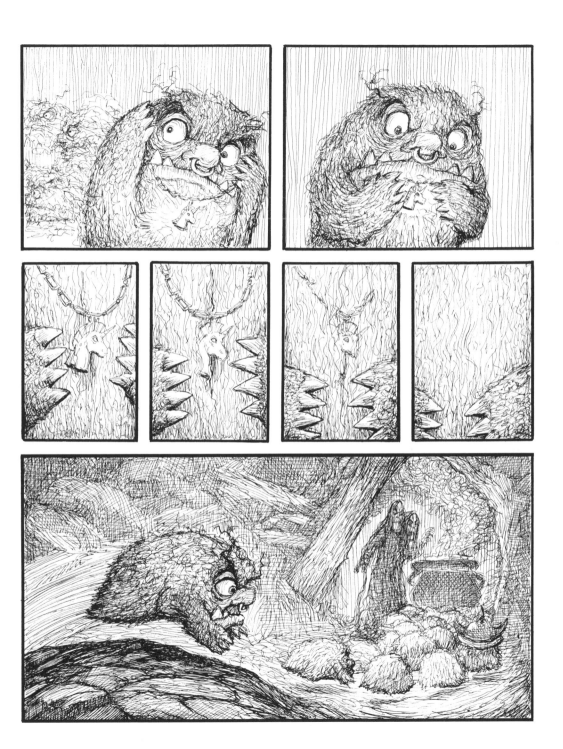

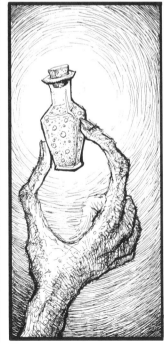

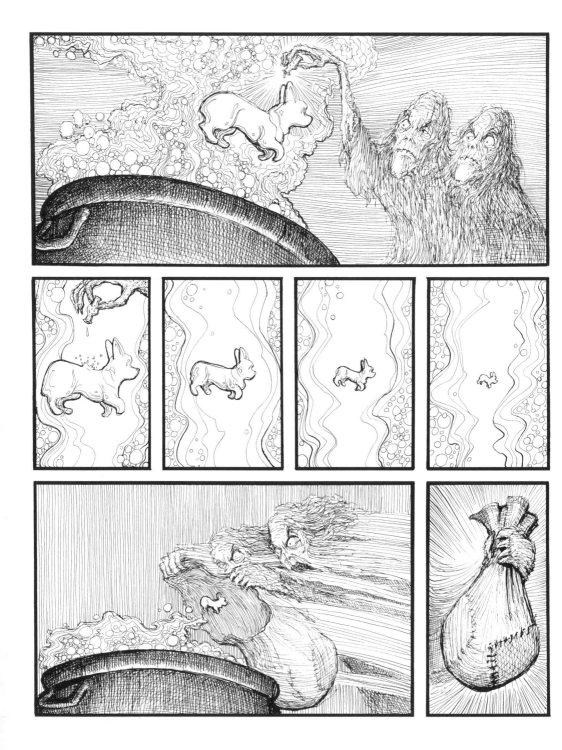

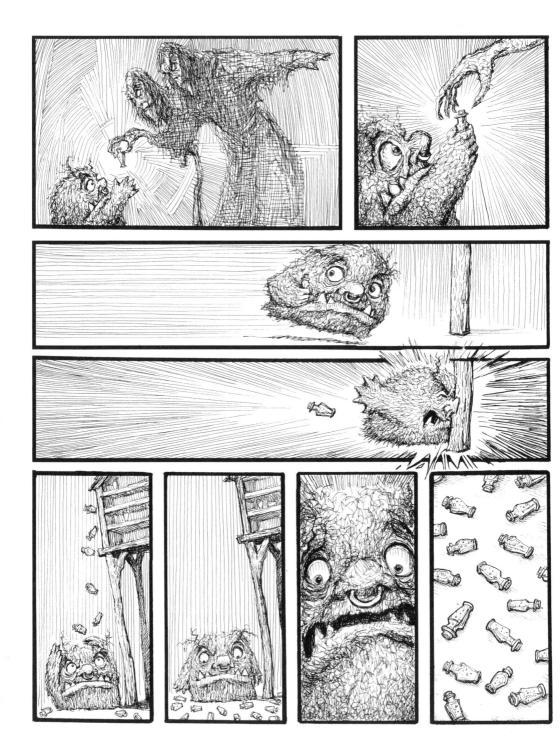

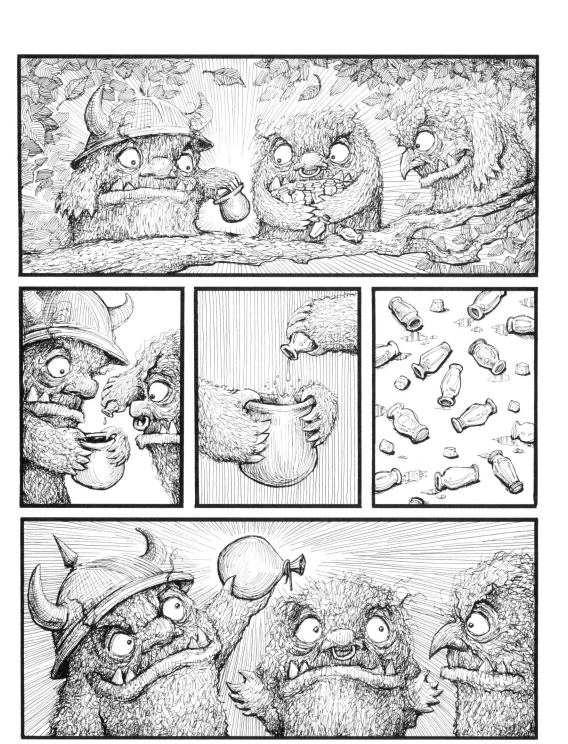

41

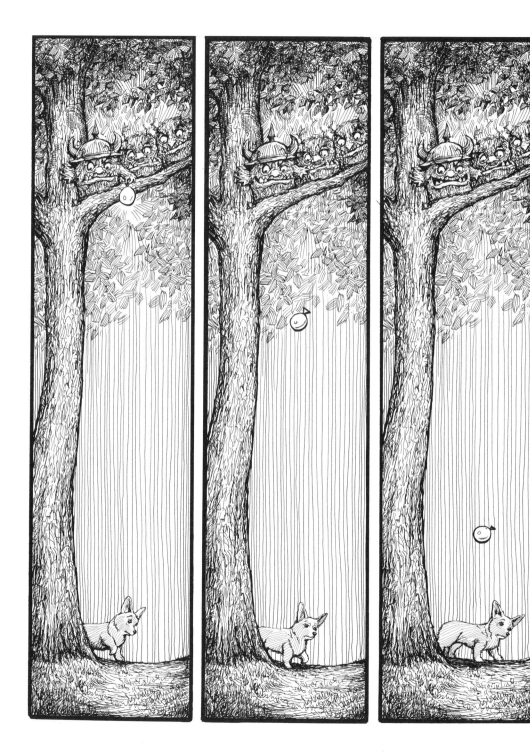

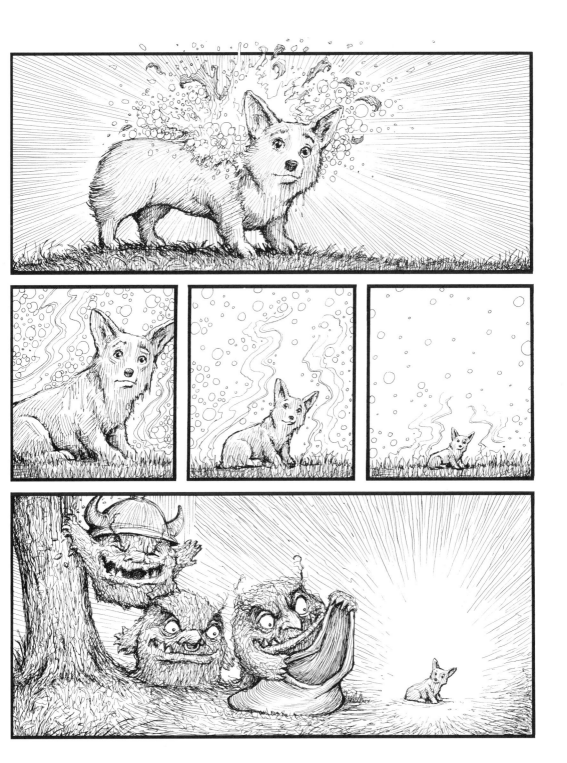

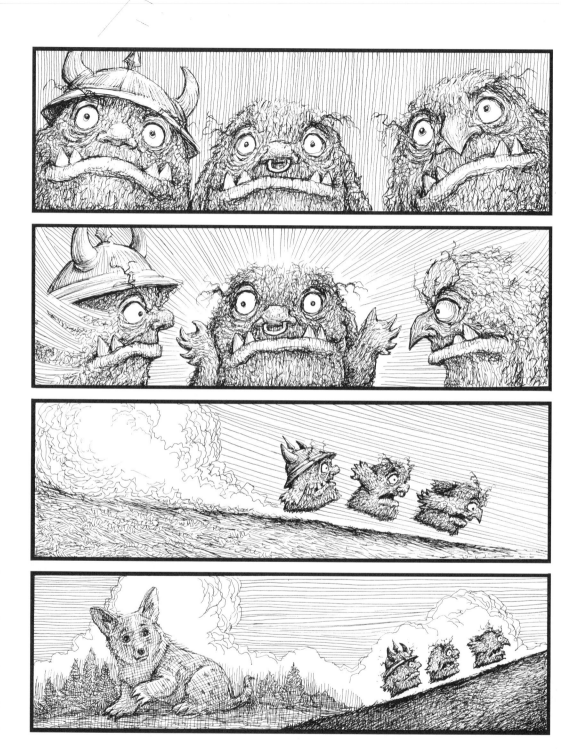

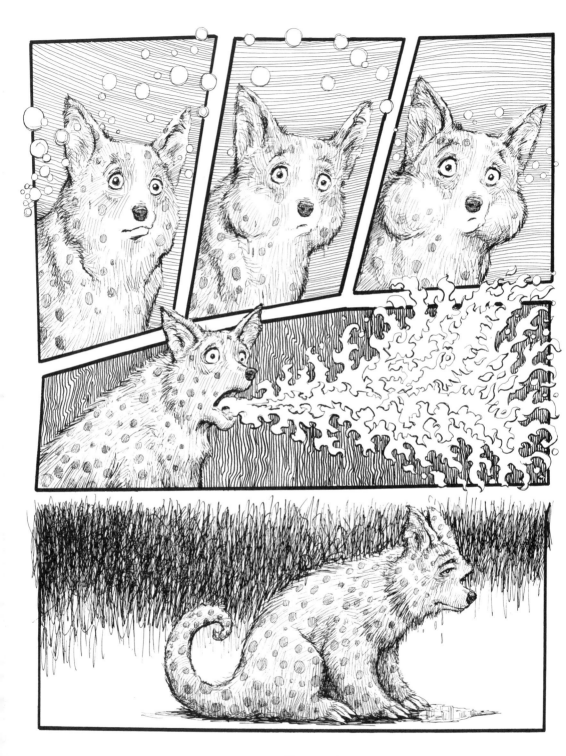

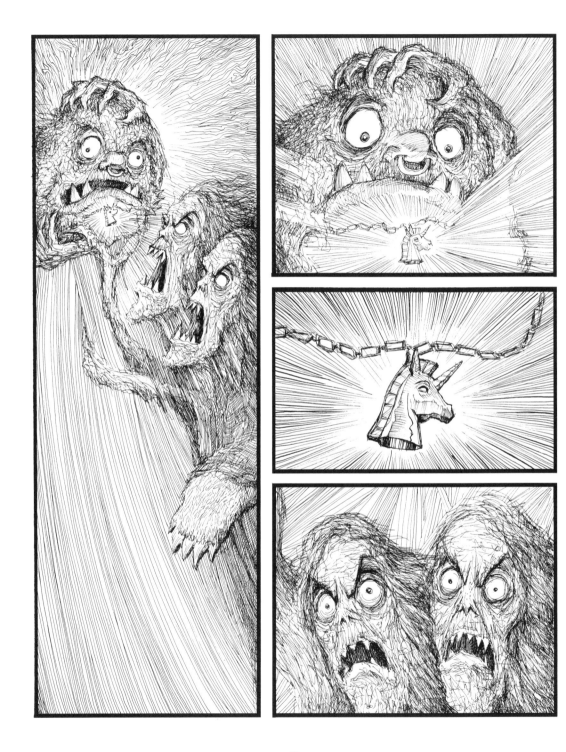

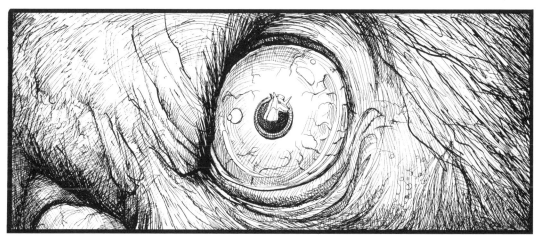

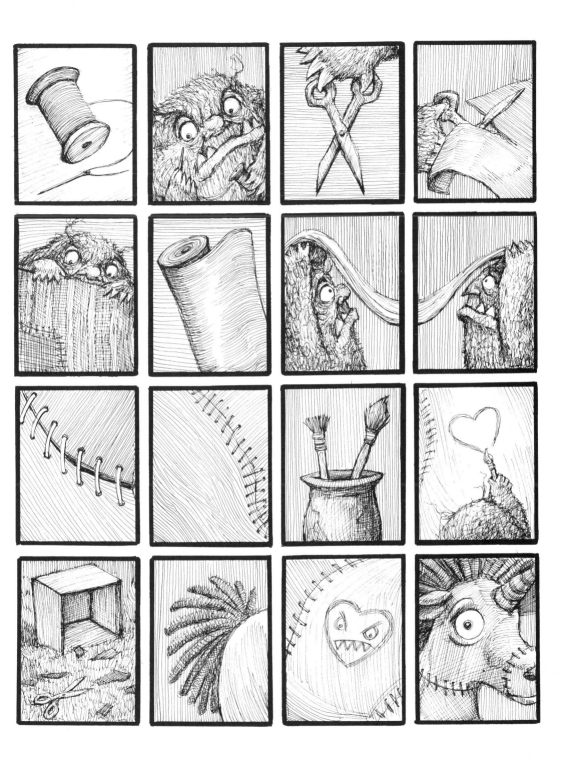

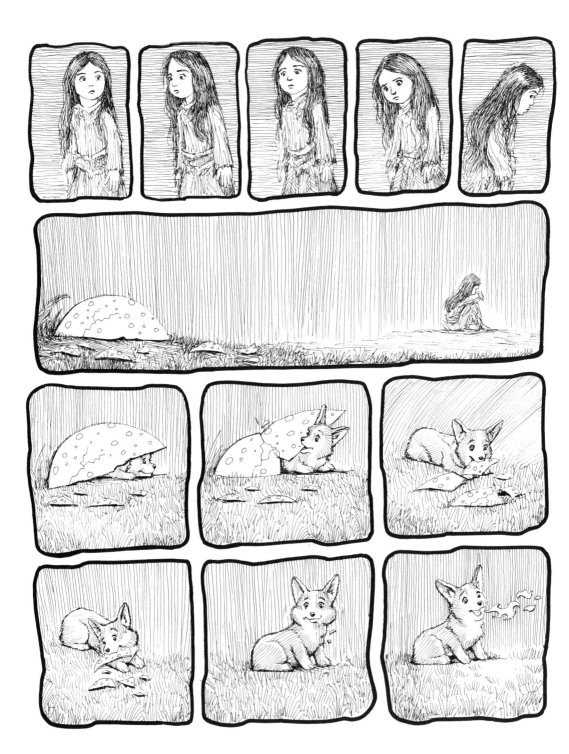

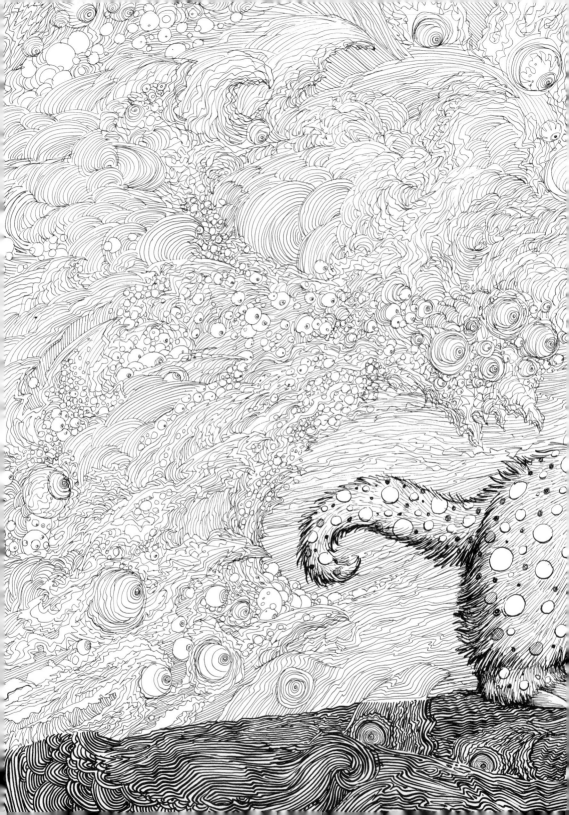

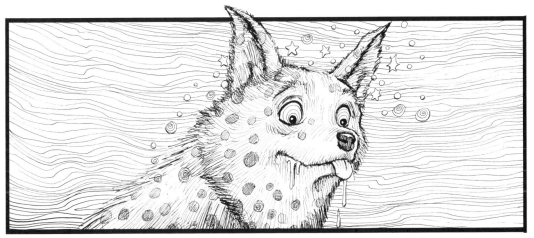

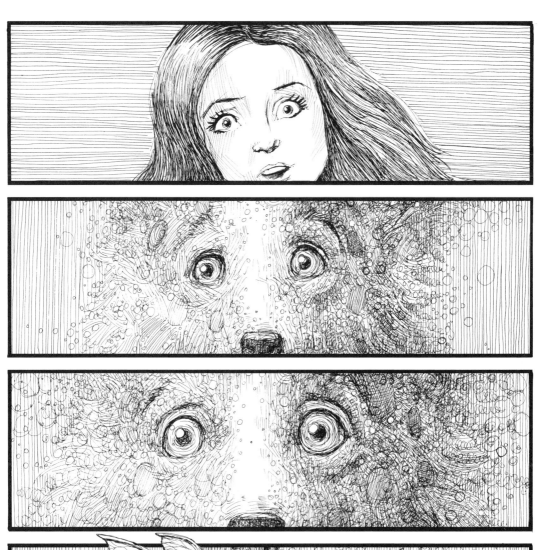

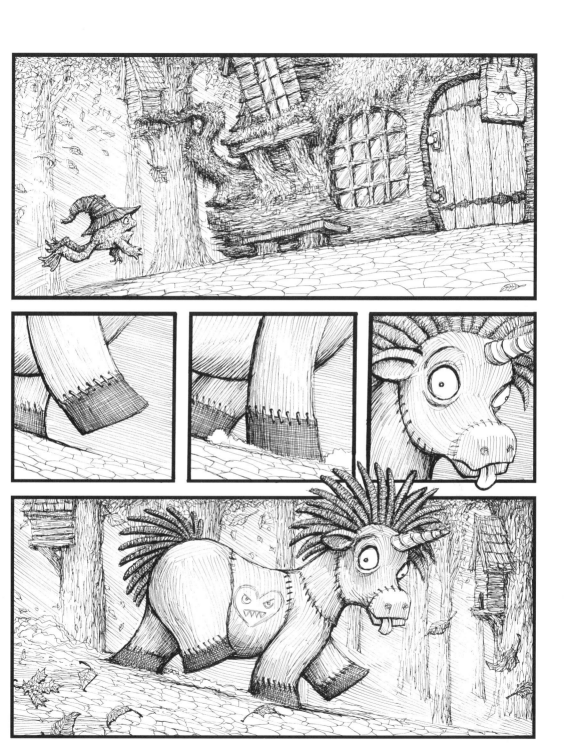

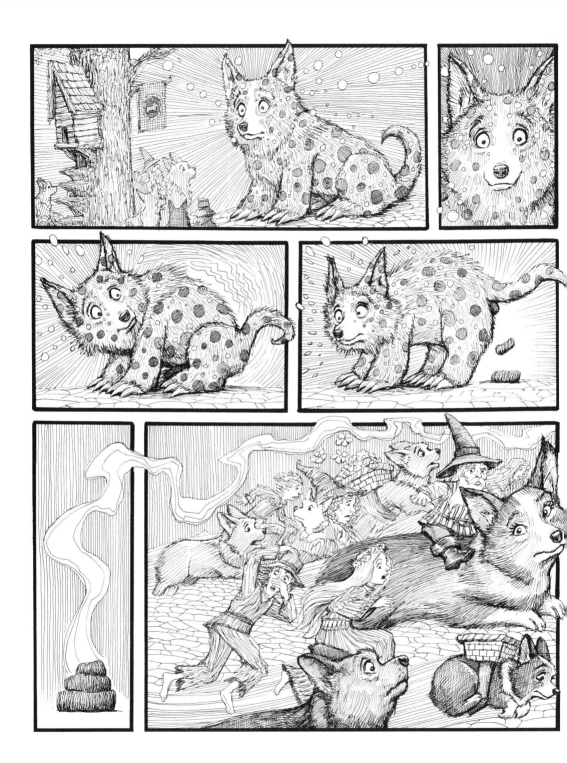

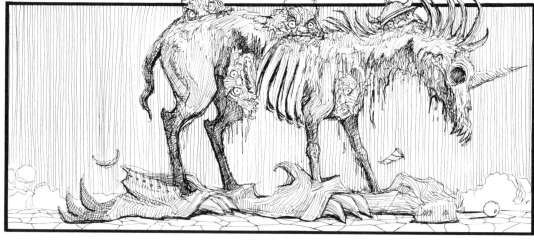

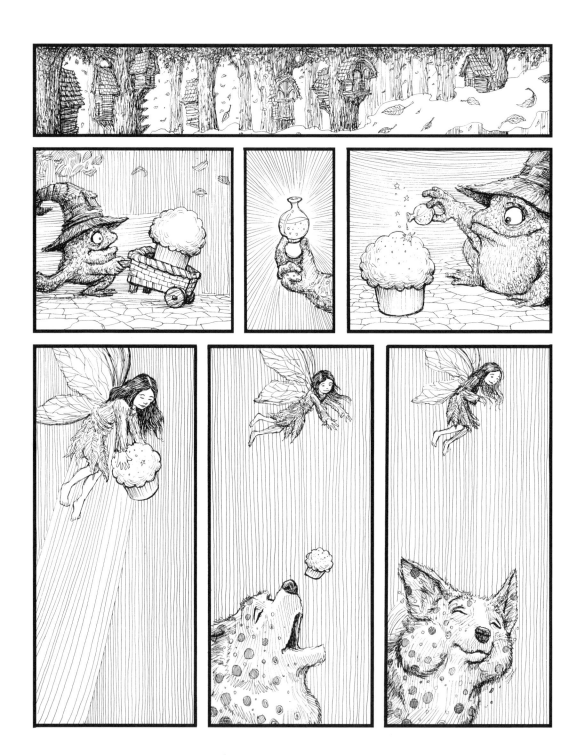

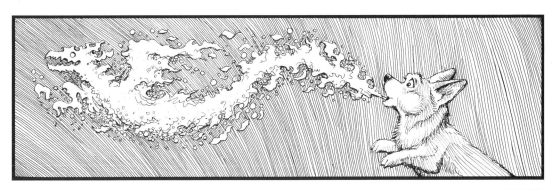

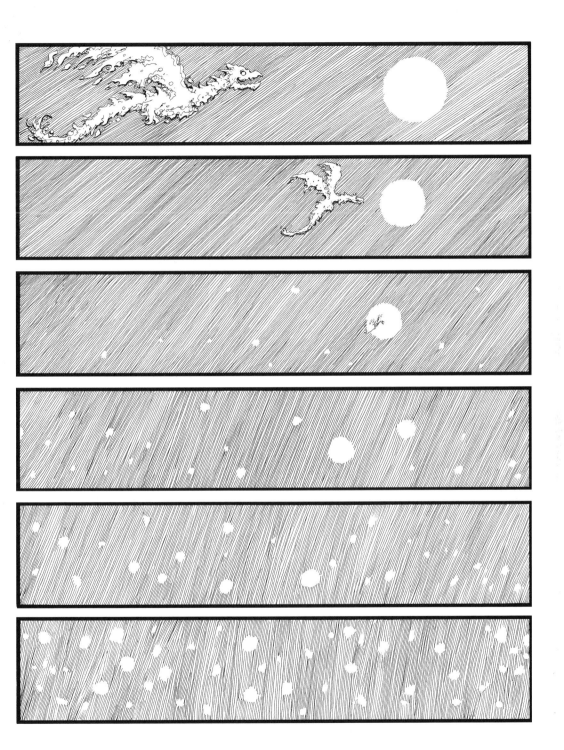

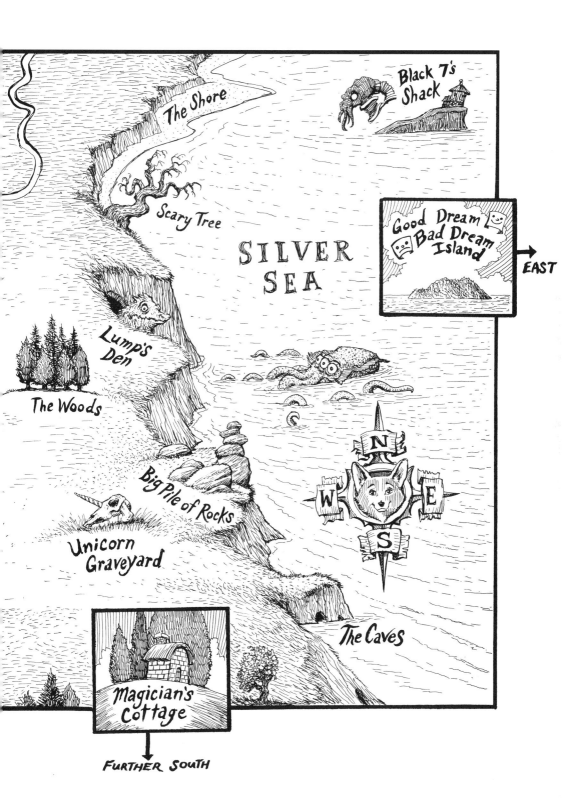

The Shore

Black 7's Shack

Scary Tree

SILVER SEA

Good Dream
Bad Dream
Island

EAST

Lump's Den

The Woods

N

W E

S

Big Pile of Rocks

Unicorn Graveyard

The Caves

Magician's Cottage

FURTHER SOUTH

CHARACTERS

IVY Sprout's best friend and caretaker. Ivy found Sprout when they were both very young. As with many Mollies, Ivy will grow up alongside her Korgi cub, who helps her realize her potential. Ivy spends a lot of time caring for Sprout, helping out in the Korgi community, and using her flying ability to patrol the outer edges of surrounding lands.

SPROUT Ivy's Korgi cub and best friend. Even though Sprout is young, he possesses the great talent of fire-breathing, a rare skill that has not been seen in a Korgi for many generations. Sprout is a curious cub who enjoys exploring the lands surrounding Korgi Hollow with Ivy. He also has a great passion for food!

WART Having lived in Korgi Hollow for a long time, Wart collects books and is the town's historian, scroll keeper, and librarian. He also counsels many of the Hollow's leaders, advising on important matters that concern the growth and safety of the village.

OTTO Living just outside the border of Korgi Hollow in the Burrow community, Otto practices his archery skills every day. He has a history of playing practical jokes with his good friends Ivy and Sprout.

CREEPHOG Dirty, stinky and, well…creepy are a few of the words to describe these creatures. Creephogs like to dwell under ground or be partially buried in dirt, which they also like to eat. They are natural diggers, which makes them tough to spot. They are excellent spies. That said, their small brains and constant bickering get in the way of retaining much information.

SCARLETT A FRIEND OF LUMP WHO ENJOYS SINGING. SHE IS OLDER THAN LUMP AND HELPED LOOK AFTER HIM AS HE GREW UP IN THE OCEANSIDE CAVE.

DEROG-GLAW THIS TWO-HEADED MONSTER IS THE RESULT OF TWO EVIL PRINCES (ONE NAMED DEROG, THE OTHER NAMED GLAW) WHOSE CAULDRON WENT AWRY AND EXPLODED WHEN THEY WERE USING POTIONS THAT WOULD HELP REVEAL THEIR ESCAPED KORGI PRISONERS. WHEN THE MAGIC BACKFIRED, DEROG AND GLAW WERE FUSED TOGETHER INTO A HIDEOUS CREATURE BURIED IN THE DUNGEON BELOW THE COLLAPSED KINGDOM. OVER MANY, MANY YEARS, DEROG-GLAW HAVE USED THEIR MIND CONTROL OVER THE CREEPHOGS, WHO HAVE NO CHOICE BUT TO SERVE THEIR MASTER AND HELP IT RECOVER. THE ONLY WAY DEROG-GLAW CAN SPLIT AND BECOME TWO AGAIN IS BY DRINKING THE BLOOD OF A FIRE-BREATHING KORGI.

LUMP A FRIEND TO ALL THE MOLLIES AND KORGIS, LUMP TRIES TO HELP THEM IN ANY WAY HE CAN. THIS IS SOMETIMES DIFFICULT, AS HE IS VERY CLUMSY AND EASILY SCARED. LUMP WAS ABANDONED WHEN HE WAS A YOUNG DRAGON BECAUSE HE CANNOT BREATHE FIRE AND DOESN'T HAVE WINGS. HE GREW UP LIVING IN A CAVE ALONG THE COAST OF THE SILVER SEA.

MOLLIES & KORGIS MOLLIES USED TO BE A TINY, LAZY GROUP OF WOODLAND FOLK. THIS CHANGED WHEN THE CUTE AND FUZZY KORGIS CAME TO LIVE WITH THEM. SINCE THEN, THE MOLLIES, WHILE STILL SMALL, ARE FULL OF LIFE AND ENERGY. KORGIS ARE FUZZY ANIMALS WITH BIG EARS, BIG SMILES, AND EVEN BIGGER HEARTS THAT HAVE THE SPECIAL ABILITY TO HELP THOSE AROUND THEM BY THEIR VERY PRESENCE. OFTEN, THOSE IN THE COMPANY OF KORGIS DISCOVER POWERS THEY DIDN'T KNOW THEY HAD, SUCH AS THE ABILITY TO FLY OR BUILD ELABORATE THINGS.

GALLUMP

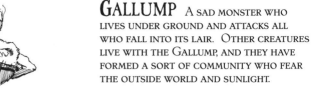A SAD MONSTER WHO LIVES UNDER GROUND AND ATTACKS ALL WHO FALL INTO ITS LAIR. OTHER CREATURES LIVE WITH THE GALLUMP, AND THEY HAVE FORMED A SORT OF COMMUNITY WHO FEAR THE OUTSIDE WORLD AND SUNLIGHT.

LIEUTENANT

A CREATURE WHO OFTEN KEEPS COMPANY WITH THE GALLUMP. HE GOT HIS SPACE OUTFIT BY LOOTING THE CRASHED ALIEN SHIP THAT LOOMS ABOVE THE GALLUMP'S LAIR.

KNICK & NACK

SMALL TWIN SNAILS WHO ARE OFTEN SEEN AROUND THE HOLLOW. THEY LIKE RACING EACH OTHER, ROWING BOATS ALONG THE CREEKS, AND TELLING SCARY STORIES.

BLACK 7

A MAROONED ALIEN WHOSE SHIP CRASHED LONG AGO ON THE BORDERING LANDS OF KORGI HOLLOW.

BOTS
REMOTE-CONTROLLED TOYS BUILT AND COLLECTED BY BLACK 7.

FIRE FRIEND

As Sprout gets older and stronger, so do his powers. His ability to breathe fire has developed to the point of being able to conjure the fire into the shape of a dragon, which becomes a helper. Sprout is only able to do this, however, when he hears his favorite music.

RAMSEY

Larger than any two Creephogs combined, Ramsey is the chief of the Creephog gang. He has a great love of Korgis and fluffy toys, which he keeps secret from Derog-Glaw and the other Creephogs.

DINGO, RINGO, AND BINGO

Three Creephogs who often work together. Dingo wears an ancient armored helmet, Ringo mixes up the potions, and Bingo does not talk.

UNDEAD UNICORN AND DISGUISE COSTUME

LONG AGO, UNICORNS USED TO ROAM FREE AND TERRORIZE THE LANDS, SPREADING PANIC AND PARANOIA WITH THEIR WICKED WAYS. NOW, AFTER OBTAINING AN OLD UNICORN TALISMAN, THE AWFUL DEROG-GLAW IS ABLE TO BRING ONE OF THESE ANCIENT CREATURES BACK FROM THE GRAVE. THE PLAN IS TO DISGUISE THE UNDEAD UNICORN IN A CLOWN COSTUME FILLED WITH CREEPHOG WARRIORS, THEN ROLL INTO KORGI HOLLOW WHERE THE CREEPHOGS WILL SNEAK OUT AND CAPTURE SPROUT FOR THEIR MASTER...A PERFECT PLAN THAT CANNOT GO WRONG.

GIANT SPROUT

AFTER BEING POISONED BY A MIXED-UP BALLOON FILLED WITH TOO MANY POTIONS, SPROUT TRANSFORMS INTO A GIANT CREATURE WITH SPOTS AND A TAIL. THE EFFECTS ARE TEMPORARY, THOUGH, AND SPROUT IS CURED WHEN WART PROVIDES AN ANTIDOTE.